MW00743813

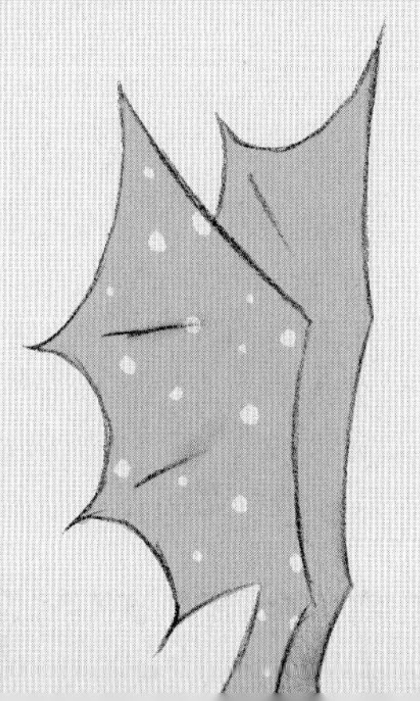

Goodnight, Dragons

by Judith L. Roth

illustrated by Pascal Lemaitre

Disney • Hyperion Books
New York

There are dragons in the forest.
No, not dragonflies.
Real dragons.

The reason I know is this—
I slept under the great chestnut tree
deep in the woods
and dreamed of dragon things.

I am called
to tame dragons.
My heart tells me so.

I gather my tools.
I pack up my traps.
I fine-tune my tricks
for dragon taming.

Into the forest,
into the trees,
with my horse and my wagon.

I'm ready.

A roar spooks my horse.
Hot gusts from above
ruffle my hair.
My heart pounds.

A smell like burnt toast
seeps through the trees.

I shake as I climb,
but I have a plan.
This is what I know—

Everyone needs a cuddle.
Maybe dragons more than most.

With a voice strong as hawksong,
I call them to me.

Come, you heartbreakers. Come, you brokenhearted.

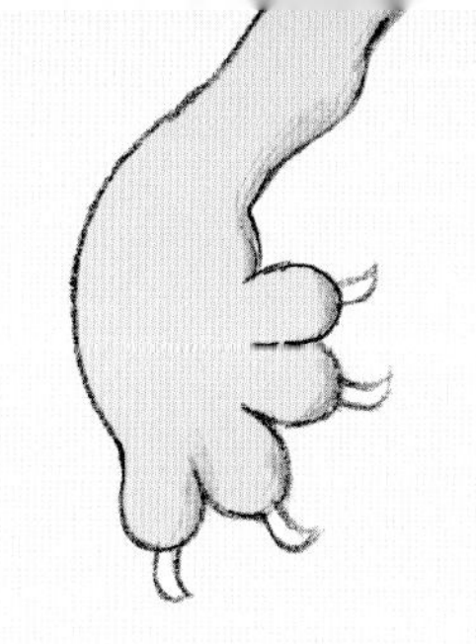

Come, put out your fire with sweet chocolate milk.

They drop from the sky

like huge, grouchy bats,

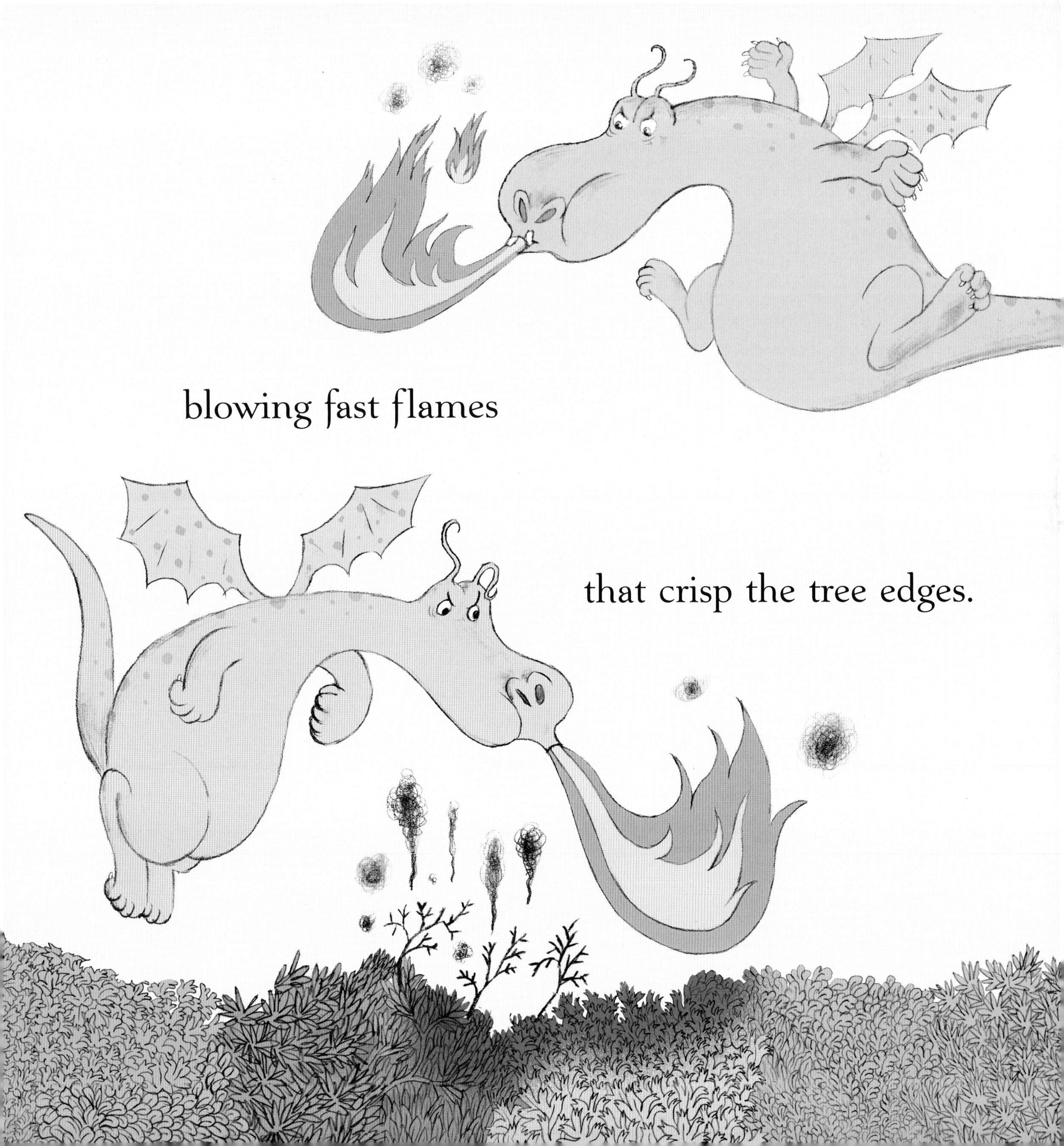

blowing fast flames

that crisp the tree edges.

But I wrap them in blankets,
soft as morning mist,
soft as summer flowers,
soft as feathered nests.

Slower now,
they stomp through the meadow
like hot, cranky rhinos,
flattening grasses,
scaring all things small.

But I settle them in clover,
gentle as springtime,
gentle as moonlight,
gentle as baby's breath.

Now, dragons, a sleepy-time treat.

Drop in the chocolate.

Add milk and a flame.
Stir up together . . .

HOT CHOCO

LATE IS BORN.

I watch the dragons

nodding in nap time,
soothed in their slumber,
tame for a time.

Maybe all a dragon needs is a cuddle.

Maybe all a dragon needs is one sweet dream.

Goodnight, dragons.

For Corey, who makes dragons come to life
—J.L.R.

For my hot chocolates: Maëlle and Manou
—P.L.

Library of Congress Cataloging-in-Publication Data

Roth, Judith L.
Goodnight, dragons / by Judith L. Roth ; illustrated by Pascal Lemaitre.—1st ed.
p. cm.
Summary: Using kindness, soft blankets, and chocolate milk, a brave child tames ferocious dragons and settles them in a clover field for a nap.
ISBN-13: 978-1-4231-4190-7
ISBN-10: 1-4231-4190-3
[1. Dragons—Fiction. 2. Naps (Sleep)—Fiction.] I. Lemaitre, Pascal, ill. II. Title.
PZ7.R72787Goo 2012
[E]—dc22 2011018185

3 5 7 9 10 8 6 4 2
G615-7693-2-12174
Printed in China
This book is set in Nevia
The art was created in pencil with digital color
Book design by Whitney Manger
Reinforced binding
Visit www.disneyhyperionbooks.com